"I like to read through each issue of *wildness* thinking about how much attention these editors give to organizing the work into one collaborative, unfolding experience."

— Justin Phillip REED

Winner of the 2018 National Book Award for Poetry

wildness, a literary journal

OMNIBUS 2015-19

wildness, a journal released quarterly by Platypus Press (an independent publisher of poetry, fiction, and narrative non-fiction), was established in 2015 and is based in Shropshire, England.

. . .

Journal Editors   Michelle TUDOR
                   Peter BARNFATHER

Contact   enquiries@platypuspress.co.uk

. . .

wildness, Omnibus 2015-19 © Platypus Press, 2019
All works copyrighted to the individual authors.
All works used by permission. All rights reserved.

ISBN 978-1-913007-04-1

Cover and interior design by Peter BARNFATHER
Type set in Bergamo Pro, FontSite Inc.
Printed & bound by Clays Ltd, Elcograf S.p.A.

WILDNESS

omnibus
2015-19

POETRY

Marco YAN	1	Two Leaves
Dalton DAY	2	Inject / Extract / Inject / Extract
Maggie SMITH	3	Lacrimae
Abigail CHABITNOY	5	Quliyangua'uciikamken
Shastra DEO	8	Scorched Earth
Geffrey DAVIS	10	Self-Portrait with Headwaters
Bethany SWANN	13	Ode to an Aviatrix
Mary MUSSMAN	15	Stonefruit Season
Irène MATHIEU	17	long distance
Theophilus KWEK	20	My Grandfather Visits Pyongyang
Chen CHEN	22	A Favorite Room
Raena SHIRALI	23	conjuring anew
Peter LABERGE	26	Sagittarius
S. Erin BATISTE	27	Date Night
Kyle DACUYAN	29	I Am No Angeleno
Anis MOJGANI	31	In May she came, in May she stayed, in May she was gone
Jeremy RADIN	35	On the Two Year Anniversary of Your Death
Omar SAKR	37	The Exhibition of Autobiography
Janel PINEDA	38	In Another Life
Hanif ABDURRAQIB	40	None of My Vices Are Violent Enough to Undo Remembering

cont.

Tariq LUTHUN	43	Ḥarb (*or* On Waging War in Spite of God)
K-Ming CHANG	45	Lone wolf narrative
Clint SMITH	47	When people say, "we have made it through worse before"
Ruth AWAD	48	Moral Inventory
Leila CHATTI	49	Postcard from Gone

NON-FICTION

Nina Li COOMES	51	On Jellyfish
David ROMPF	57	Yesterday Is a Wild Parrot
An UONG	67	My Sometimes Vietnamese

FICTION

Patricia PATTERSON	77	Eucharist
Sylvia WATANABE	87	Days
	95	Contributors

POETRY

Two Leaves

Marco YAN

One abrades another, in awe, on the surface,
grapples, losing some green, some soft yellow.

Good leaves don't fall easy on foreign water
or sink into the gurgling mouths of koi—

so I believed—the night I ran to where you were,
leaping over a pothole scratched open by ice.

Have you ever stooped to study a leaf,
its venation bleached like bones in a bird's foot?

I still don't know if I'm made for water,
made of thoughts, or thoughtlessness, to drift—where?

You're no longer a leaf, more like a fish skipping,
now legs walking away. Nature loves reversals.

I'm held in this blue circumference, stagnant, drying,
wanting to freeze a light.

Inject / Extract / Inject / Extract

Dalton DAY

You say you feel like a needle, dropped.

You don't say that, exactly, but you feel that, exactly.

Swollen is not what we ever mean.

Moon, instead.

Moon, like, *Moon* the first time we ever made it there
    & joy was said but fear wasn't.

The body can't attack itself.

I don't say that, exactly, but I believe that, exactly?

I don't believe that, exactly, but the wind
    wants to make a sound when it moves through you.

I can't hear it.

The body does what it does without asking.

I'm covered in hands, *Mountain*,
    & now only some of them are yours.

Lacrimae

Maggie SMITH

Green dashes for grassland, brown dots
for desert, solid blue for water—

the children's atlas is all simulacra,
from the Latin for *likeness*, which always

reminds me of *lacrimae*, Latin for *tears*.
That's the rickety bridge my brain makes

over the river, or the kinked blue line
that stands for it. What a landscape

in the symbolic distance: dark green
lollipops for deciduous forest,

a cluster of black carats for mountains.
Once, doing dishes, I overheard

my children bickering about metaphysics
in the next room. The three-year-old

said, *Everything is true*, and his older
sister countered, *Do you mean real?*

wildness literary journal

When I think *likeness*, I think
tears—blue always for water, blue

running through and under everything.

Quliyangua'uciikamken

Abigail CHABITNOY

The wind is not a river.

I am afraid of most waters but some days
I too desire drowning—
                        drop my eye
below the sight.

"Hello blackwater."

I wish some days
I could put on my sister's skin
                        to see the body
other than my death.

What if this river is wind? I don't really know
about sharks and salmon after all.

        swim. not swim. one must take care
        entering any body of modest depth.

I will tell you a story.

I feel more mouth than maw these days
more bird than fish.

wildness literary journal

What we're missing, waves: an exact measurement
of distance
       a body in context
       an appreciation for the size
of a full grown walrus.

One dies soon.

It used to be these events occurred
hundreds of years
apart.

The story goes and grows until no bigger than a harbor
seal,
   small and
       spotted
in need of saving and   native
    to the wrong waters.

Blackwater, bad weather.

How do you know if you're holding walrus
or elephant?
     snow or
ash?
  potsherd
       or cranial
plate?

What if this wind is river?

Yaatiini, akgua'aq, emerpak cali aqllangenguartuq.

The last few days have been windy.

wildness literary journal

Scorched Earth

Shastra DEO

For a long time I used to dream about smoke
swirling in an empty room. The wood
stumps we set to burn in the fireplace: crumbled

into ash and embers; transformed. The body
and the space it occupies: set alight.
The body and the space it occupied: dispersed.

Exploded. Illuminated—like dust particles
in a shaft of light. The smoke still rises; the scent of scorch
lingers, trapped, despite the passing of years.

+

The more I think about your body, the more I know
it is no longer your own: your heart is a house
with the doors left open; your brain is the basement

filled with smoke. The skeleton hidden under the flesh
of the floorboards. A stranger roaming the hallways, a
dappled shadow splashed on the wall, flickering in the firelight.

+

I remember peeling peaches in the gloaming,
the juice sluicing down your chin. The moths
threw themselves onto the bonfire and I knew what it was

to burn: your eyes alight and gleaming,
insects swirling a crown around your skull.
The world was on fire and your fingers

popped as you pressed your palms over the whites
of my eyes, the beat of your heart like
an unlatched door: open, shut, open.

Self-Portrait with Headwaters

Geffrey DAVIS

My father failed to let our family eat and yet, for years, remained beautiful and resilient to me. Some call it addiction. So now I fear and feign what's spring-fed about hunger, what's dark about my thirst. Run-off watersheds go low and deadly warm for fish, according to shifts in season, but the numbed vein of a spring will bless a river's biota with refuge only the cold can provide.

*

Like Carbon Glacier, sometimes what sustains us looks more dingy than dangerous up close. A dirty discharge carves for miles before becoming the scenic Carbon River with its sediment-rich current and chrome salmon fortified through their passage back from the deep obscurity of the Pacific. During my most reckless autumn, I escaped the city and ascended an icy trail to its headwaters, coatless. When I arrived neither cold nor hungry and found an ugliness that did little to quiet my stubborn search for a myth to solve for worry, I returned to the river's singular direction—: everything altered, but nothing complete.

*

I am the only member of my clan to kill something from the Mississippi, to dangle a barbed question into that legacy:—What portion of this do I wish to be true? With a drainage that begins in northern Minnesota, the River snakes thousands of miles between Rocky and Appalachian Mountains, growing by gathering a part of its fluid force from more than half the US states, before muddying into the Delta South. I know: the water that school told me to equate with a low-down, dirty terror has long since been divided and dispelled by the Gulf—so why then, while fishing shores of the Mississippi, do I feel and fear hooking a diaspora of drowned faces?

*

As a child I would climb into the warm mouth of my parents' bed, trembled by the Sunday sermon, ready to beg away a short life of going left:—sins of the curious son, desires of the greedy goat, accidents of the forgetful brother. By sixteen, after sex, I had discovered too many appetites for which to atone. What could I choose but call the spirit of that first prayer—"Keep me with You"—a false course. Anyway, weren't we designed for dispersal, to be diminished by the grave thirst of the fields that lie below? And who would deny the fertility of some absences? I do, however, love the glamor of an eddy, its unresolved meander, its agile queering of the current's dumb flow. And I confess my gluttony for the immediate, so give me a break—or a gentler gradient—: a little more time to soak in all this contact falling away. How much worse should I be at confluence? How many blues must be banished to the bleary basin of memory? So it goes. So we go. And we go.

Sundown, with maps and flow charts spread around the living-room floor, *I'm trying to distinguish the river's source from its parts—which should show me how best to approach tomorrow's fishing.* From the couch, L smiles with more permission than gentle teasing, so I continue: *For instance, the Sol Duc collects numerous tributaries before merging with the Bogachiel to become the Quileute—: and then, near La Push, all that gathering loses itself inside the vast Pacific.* L leans over my shoulder, her hair smelling slightly of the lavender wash she uses to bathe our boy's body before bed, her practiced *hmm* buoyed lovingly in the bay of my curiosity. *And although it originates up in the Olympic Mountains, north of the High Divide, a lack of glaciers at stream headwaters keeps its habitat consistent:—and so the Sol Duc is one of few rivers on the Peninsula to support all major species of migratory fish.* Though not an angler herself, L knows how I long most to hold the elusive steelhead in these coastal hands. Time and again I perform this ceremony—part memory, part prayer—and against what light remains, it occurs to me, *I don't understand the why of my craving to locate certain corridors through which the right water passes—to make contact less impossible between bodies otherwise drifting apart.* Once more, I've lingered long beyond the body's deep bell for sleep, so L rises into the dark's soft extinction, and I follow—: the comfort of her tired steps sounding within my blind but promised reach.

Ode to an Aviatrix

Bethany SWANN

for Katherine Sui Fun Cheung

Whole continents teem with your static
loveliness. Pieces of sky sugar down

in excelsis, touch airways you've hallowed
& conquered in wingspan, red-tipped dust.

As the cockpit sun skids down your arm,
dear aviatrix, we see the hollows of your face

framed in surfaces: island shallows   blue, isometric;
mountaintops shagged in ice.

And we know Ascension is this: the breaking

of day around us, pulsing the way a new heart
might pulse—or pivot on its transatlantic axis.

But things have a way of turning red
when you'd least expect: coordinates go

missing, a flare gun loses its savory, vines
trawl across terminals, make imposing demands.

At dusk, these runways unfurl their dark:

skein of veins, a map unspooling
at the base of your flawless skull.

Stonefruit Season

Mary MUSSMAN

Movements of chairs over the floorboards
resound from the upstairs window,
sent off
        like starlings

from the sanity of our family:

        our grandmother lived for nine decades.

She would use walnuts to smooth out nicks left
in the wood,

its oil rich and fragrant

when the coroner opened the crevices
of her body
        and found deposits of mercury.

Now is not the time for explanations—
        follow me.

Wait in the library,
leaf through this text:

wildness literary journal

"Penumbra is the simplest translation
of *la pénombre*, since the Latin lingers behind both words

      (almost-shadow / *paene-umbra*)."

Some other time, you'll stumble across it
in a ghost story as "semi-darkness."

The coffee in your mug will be
cooled, the tea in mine still steaming.

long distance

Irène MATHIEU

driving in early winter to my love who lives two states away
sprays of blackbirds fling across the slough tucked into the curve of an exit ramp
where Pennsylvania gives way to Delaware, of sheared cornfields, of farmhouses with
their splintered mouths opening to mudfields puddled with the palm of the sky, Lenape
land, fields covered in defeated stalks like small pyres pointing heavenward, clouds
sworn to mundane iridescence.

time spells out the movement of all matter, but only matter.

to watch a day end: make your way through pink-skied country
how to hold the skeletons of poplars and power lines in the mind as they mark the miles—
here Maryland, here trees stripped of their flesh—

the road opens up the land and we ask
if we were meant to see it this way.

closer to heaven the geese are pointing southward and it seems a small miracle of
organization, though maybe every creature moves as diligently toward warmth as I do
now. humans haven't yet learned how not to kill ourselves a little each time we move.

now the moon is a bright coin, now a single planet beckons, hypnotizes, lantern-like,
maybe more beautiful than this one if we could set our hot feet on it. we call a thing
lovely only after we have broken it.

confused animal I am, mesmerized by the goldening horizon, my movements as purposeful as
a moth's when viewed from a satellite that ribbons the earth for decades.
our heat-seeking will be the death of us—the same banality of a dozen moths' velvety
bodies impaled on my car's headlights

and at the end of these hours

there will be a glass of wine, some bread, the deep and satisfied stretch of my love's
laughter over me. the interstate behind me will not be filled in my mind with fur and
smears of oil and the entrails of unlucky deer we leave in our wake.

for my father as a child it was the small magic of Christmas-lit homes that unstrung him down to his bright core; for my mother, the awakening in a scalding shower. we seem not to want for much, but oh, how even this much has taken! I think I love myself more than I love the land, and that may be my greatest grief one hundred years from now.

the presumptuousness of asking forgiveness in advance——of the reddening sky, of my grandchildren. the misguided thought that there is penance in a poem.
here is the Bay bridge, here the choppy Chesapeake waters, here the Virginia I love to love from behind glass, gulls dipping with each pulsing brake light predictable as a person's heartbeat.

love, pick something to sacrifice. by which I mean I want to be both human and an animal worthy of this speck of dust.

My Grandfather Visits Pyongyang

Theophilus KWEK

Too late, we find among his photographs
A kingdom mostly dreamed of,

Its absurd architecture where
He alighted some time in October.

Frame after frame resists comparison.
There isn't a place we've seen

That stands as still, or with the same intent
Raises its glass towards heaven,

All normalcy locked within a sound
These pictures don't contain—a pitch rung

In the earth's confines, too low
For human hearing. Friends tell us to allow

Ourselves the time it takes
To grieve, or whatever brings us back

To last year's long continuum,
But something stays the eye. How in some

Perspectives he's already gone,
Gone from the boulevards where wide-crowned

Trees fill up the viewfinder,
And men and women in work clothes hover

Outside our field of vision. He's
Somewhere else entirely, now close,

Now looking in, the disappearance
Nothing more than a trick of the lens,

Though we fall for it again and again.
How like him, we think,

Then catch ourselves. The pages turn
On their own impulse in our hands.

A Favorite Room

Chen CHEN

Down the sideways face, through the dilapidated waterfall,
we entered late afternoon's house
& a favorite room: the room of the butterfly skeleton.

Intricate, delicate, somehow not an ounce of tragic.
So beautiful we thought we could have perfect
unswollen gums, be less predictable
gay men, obsessed with our mothers.

It whispered: the new year will bring more coffee flavors,
& sodas, overall more beverage-related upheavals.

It advised us never to buy anything
fresh again, & thus we could be just like it—

Never misspelling a state capital.
Never missing a coworker's birthday.
Always just pretending to be dead.

conjuring anew

Raena SHIRALI

you don't know why you feel the urge to tell him
in his absence you collect debris :   ripped

envelopes, the coin he pressed against your nipple
to see how hard you'd shiver

you thought then you knew the cold. you thought then
your spikes were weapons

+

so you are a spine with several protrusions

that doesn't make you unlovable

+

remind yourself :   your situation is only negative
if you consider it in contrast to pastels :   the sky almost
a dusting of pink, his thumb & forefinger
hooked around your earlobe

+

he calls you *paint speckled*
but means *rust ridden*. he calls you *corrugated*

but you're already on your back. you're too fair
to be : too dark to be :

+

if you took all the cloud's colors at dusk & mixed them together
you'd get brown, anyway. in this way, you are at the center
of the sky—& he is another object
headed straight toward it

+

or this is no firmament, but a landfill

+

you may be just another artifact
kept in an old shoebox—a love letter he takes out
after several glasses, reads less-than-fondly

+

it's hard, isn't it, to look at yourself

without a mirror : without a man

\+

if you're ready for the recipe, take out your largest
porcelain bowl. gather scents you feel are particularly

you : rosemary, lavender, rain soaked cigarettes, dark
ripe sweat. let them sit with each other

in the half light by a lace curtain
resist the urge to mix. resist the urge

to make any blooming of your simplest parts

\+

at least, if you're going to be a cold, left thing
you can call yourself *spica*

\+

at least, once you're cold & left
you can call yourself *anything*

wildness literary journal

Sagittarius

Peter LaBerge

It is comforting to know
the man will replace
a body of similar size

                    of similar intent, promise
                    and so-on—I can
                    nearly draw a line in snow

from him I have
not met to him of my day—
him I dare not say

                    because he is not yet
                    real. I am satisfied to line
                    the mind with stones

to announce the heat
will happen somewhere
around here. But no one

                    can predict the cold,
                    the body it will bring. Try
                    as I might, I know

I could not know
every part of winter
before he has come.

Date Night

S. Erin BATISTE

It's Saturday again and soon the streets
of Old Town will be littered with lovers.

The autumn air will thicken with sugary
coffees, cream sauces, and seared meats

drawing out the lacquer-eyed couples.
Their palms weaving tightly together,

like a loom, they will limbo under string
lights: entire scene awash in wanting.

South of Union Avenue, my telephone
only reflects back the same indifferent

blackness as the September sky. Full of
pinot and bored with staring at the long

shadow engraved on the dinner chair
opposite mine, I trick my body early

into its usual flannel and solid cotton.
Desperate for something to hold,

wildness literary journal

I raise my sleepy window shade and
a dollop of stars show themselves.

I imagine the constellation as arms, whole
galaxies coalesced, ready to embrace.

I Am No Angeleno

Kyle DACUYAN

I'm a stranger here. I like that. My body
clock is ticking three hours in the future.
I wake before the news, I have pre-dawn
with the mountains. This makes me feel
if not invincible, at least not so impatiently
human. My friend in Silver Lake says
everyone here lives in the Very Right Now.
Which I think is a consequence of the constant
summer. Also his specious and rather
narrow views of *everyone* and *here*. I don't know
that there is anywhere I have an everyone.
More I am a herd of one, the calculus in my brain,
alienating and elsewhere, a sugar-high child
who won't accept the off-switch. A year ago,
a lover ago, everywhere I looked I thought
there was no beauty I could again belong to.
And now I see that what is beautiful
is what precisely I have nothing to do with.
Like this jolie-laide duck skanking through
the reeds of Echo Park, his bill fat with stolen food.
I want to trust my own joy like that. More fully,
I mean, more thoughtlessly and sweet.
There is a man I newly love back east in the future,
whose grief I want to take each time he comes
inside me. There are times I am just about

wildness literary journal

to come when I wish that I could say the names
of everyone I've ever loved at once.
Plenty of truth should be impossible
given physics, given speech, given time
and its phallic insistence on linear forward
motion. Well. My friend in Silver Lake says
should is a word that doesn't do me any favors.
So I am here in Los Angeles, but I am also
giving myself permission to be here and here
and here in the realities I am inventing.
That is the miracle of wakefulness inside
the shut pink of your eyelids. You can latch
your sublimating heart to the wingtip of a bird.
And I am, and it is flying three thousand miles
across the heartland to light the morning's
change upon my lover's face. The light is light
I have endowed with an intention.
That he remember how deeply loved he is
out here in the past, where we are kissing
and I am walking backwards down a hall.
We hold an orange between us and sway stoned
to Arthur Russell. It is Saturday. Isn't it.
We have hours and hours with nowhere to go.

In May she came, in May she stayed, in May she was gone

Anis MOJGANI

cupping palmfuls of petals
you and I
we picked leaves of basil

gray-eyed
with owls you burst forth
bark flaking off tall trees revealing
underneath a cream color

it was the same
with your heart
under my nails
hand over the port side

dipping our fingers into an ocean of flowers

broke them over bread
and tomatoes from the roof
cut so thin like us
they trembled in the wind

I want all of your skin in my mouth at the same time

a summer with nothing to do but sit on thrones

white
as a mountain peak
the inside part of your thigh

my teeth upon it

every church bell leaning in
the direction of our wild un-wildness
the place where the sun does not reach

that the earth might use us
to feel something warm upon it

—an ocean boiling
the brass casing spent and hot
after the shell has been shot from the rifle

the launching of music into the breaking of vases

limes and avocados carried over our state lines
pushing the wagon filled with your body of birds
Mexico was a time without goddesses

our heat unbuttoning our top buttons
my body laid across the balcony to catch rain

drinking the water off of one another

wishing to sip your lip
I wished only one wife in my lifetime
wished for only my tongue on your neck

only your legs to push my mouth between
wanted husband to remain

a beautiful word for you
wanted to be husband as your mother is mother

as your sister is sister your father
is father
still

the garden of your love was a strangeness
and still I loved to lay
amongst its strange things

the cruelty you at times stretched upon me
simply because there were arrows within reach
pulling the shaft through the other side

wildness literary journal

for so long I did not know the wound
could only feel the feathers
brushing their way out of it

even after it is all done
I am learning what marriage might mean
what the ever-changing relic of self means

—bird of my heart
that is not a bird

separate of the seasons I pass through
my body remains a springtime

On the Two Year Anniversary of Your Death

Jeremy RADIN

The fiddle fig in my apartment has grown quite large, top
leaves scraping the ceiling. One leaf in the middle
of the central stalk is wide enough to sit upon, say, if one
were caught in a river & needed a raft, say the river
was astonishment, time, rushing through the stages
of impermanence. My plant is a stranger to you, papa,
you never got to meet her: my dragon, my rabbi.
I can only grieve you this way—by noticing what you will
never notice: the plant, my broadening bald spot,
the way, when it rains, the fog becomes a tallis draped over
the shoulders of the hill outside my window. How alike
we are—a pair of hunched worshippers worshipping
bad weather, turning green in the absence of sun. You
will never see the way I sway to Kreisler in the car,
his violin stitching me to history, to the mystical
bewilderment that is my birthright, my destination. You
will never notice how Kayla has begun to glow, luminous
with burgeoning purpose, unburdened by the circle she
pledged herself to. You'll never know the world without
you, how it keeps going—old women buying bread, dogs
eating butterflies, children taking a sputtering country
lovingly into their hands. I should have held you more.
I should have driven you to physical therapy, to the market,

to your mother's. I should have flown you to Austin for BBQ,
New York for belly lox, Big Sur for purple sand. I should have
told you to shave the goatee. I should have shaved it. I should
have cooked you matzo brei, chicken soup, brisket. I should
have brought you tea. I should have read to you. I should
have clutched your hands & told you & told you & told you.
There was a better son in me & you never got to meet him.
Oh pops, what brutal coil will these strange years make?
Which end of me will be the end of me? I remember how
your mustache curled into a smile, a salt & pepper wave,
the frozen bananas, the delicatessen. I guess I should prune
the fig, but I don't want to. Better, I should let it grow wild.
Better yet, let it swallow me whole. God help me,
I did what I did.

The Exhibition of Autobiography

Omar SAKR

I put history in a cabinet where it can do the least
damage. I make sure to buff it from time
to time. It won't do for it to be

less than glamorous. We keep paying for it. Maybe
this is why it lives. I am obsessed with the past
the same way a victim

is obsessed with their killer, not their body
but the origin story, the motive where
the end began. In a dream

I explain this to my mother as I throttle
her neck, and she smiles. Finally,
we are a family. I won't say

when I let go, only that I don't know how
to look to a future I am certain
doesn't include me.

Everything is changing now that I am in love.
I'm still here, still sworn to sorrow's geas,
but the exit has inched closer.

In Another Life

Janel PINEDA

The war never happened but somehow you and I
    still exist. Like obsidian,
we know only the memory of lava
    and not the explosion that created

us. Forget the gunned-down church, the burning
    flesh, the cabbage soup.
There is no bus. There is no border. There is no blood.
    There are

only sweet corn fields and mango skins. The turquoise
    house and clotheslines.
A heaping plate of pasteles and curtido waiting to be
    disappeared into our bellies.

In this life, our people are not things of silences
    but whole worlds bursting
into breath. Everywhere, there are children. Playing
    freely, clothed and clean.

Mozote does not mean massacre and flowers bloom
    in every place shoes are
left behind. My name still means truth, this time
    in a language my mouth recognizes,

in a language I know how to speak. My grandmother is
        still a storyteller although I am
not a poet. In this life, I do not have to be. This poem
        somehow still exists. It is told

in my mother's voice and she makes hurt dissolve like honey
        in hot water, manzanilla
warming the throat. You and I do not find each other
        on another continent, grasping

at each other's necks in search of home. We meet in a mercado,
        my arms overflowing
with mamey and anonas, and together we wash them
        in riverwater. We watch sunset fall over

a land we call our own and do not fear its taking.
        I bite into the fruit, mouth sucking
seed from substance, pulling its veins from between my teeth.
        Our laughter echoes

from inside the cave, one we are free to step outside of.
        We do not have to hide here.
We do not have to hide anywhere. A torogoz flies past my face
        and I do not fear its flapping.

None of My Vices Are Violent Enough to Undo Remembering

Hanif ABDURRAQIB

and it is troubling isn't it
to have a reflection

that always arrives when called
despite the steam pulling

its thick tongue along a mirror's edges
after I emerge unsanctified

from underneath the raging
showerhead

and it is really something
to love only the unseen

and still be finite
back in the golden era

a good bluesman
would have a memory

only as long as it took for the last
guitar note to drown itself

in something that burned
the throat on the dance

down and I guess that doesn't seem so
bad when you consider the times

what I'm saying is that if you're going to die
broke you might as well also

do it alone
my great great grandfather could not swim

he played guitar for coins on the juke
circuit but never parted his lips

for the drink and so when the yawning
maw of the Mississippi coughed out his

remains there was no other excuse
for what dragged him

to the water except for that which he didn't
do himself the mercy of forgetting

wildness literary journal

and in all of the pictures I have his smile
it is dark outside my window

and I see my reflection in everything I see
my reflection in the water

especially the water

Harb (*or* On Waging War in Spite of God)

Tariq LUTHUN

When piqued, boys be a bone.
Be a tantrum, a cracked tomb

of discipline exorcising itself
into the backs of boys we had
no business putting our fists
inside of. I tried so hard

to find myself in the spines of the men
who wronged me. As told by

my mother: all good is holy, while evil
finds itself in those
        who do not sleep, those
        whom lie

awake learning to write and
heed, and pray; in me, this

wired thing. My father did all he could
to be sure I was birthed with a beating
fist to go with those
        sleepless beasts, my lungs.

We find — to this day — a book
of versed calligraphy is the prettiest
flesh to make a lamb of. This
is what I will tell my son

when he is beckoned by
the bully in him,
when his scorn loses
sight of its prey. If my son develops a taste

for blood, I will blame it on
the enemies of my father and our ancestors.
One day, he will ask me about the red
in the river

of our name, where it turned.
When he does, I will have
      the same answer I did
when my parents told me to hold
      my tongue and cleanse
      my fistful

heart: *I do not know what to throw away*
when nothing belongs to me.

Lone wolf narrative

K-Ming CHANG

Take your teeth off
    the light switch. America, I'll darken
        your face by holding it
            between my thighs. America, grief
        your only stable
            currency. When a white boy shoots
    up the strip mall where my mother
        waxes white women, she calls me
from the back room   backlit
    by our altars: oranges scarred,
seedless & photos of ghosts
        taken by smoke. She tells me
    to marry soon: when the right man comes, run
the risk of wreckage: love him into
            leaving his country. This one:
        a history colonized by holes. The news
    spews tonight's casualties: motor
        accident on the highway. Another country
defrosted by bombs. Another son
    kills his mother with his father's
            gun. No mention
                of the mother's race
        though I've seen her face
    is mine. There's no disowning the white
        from bone, your body from the boat

wildness literary journal

        waiting in its blood. When another news-anchor
            says *acted alone*, my mother says
                    all knives
                        come from a drawer. All widows
              come from wars. At work
          my mother cuts bangs into a woman's blonde
                son, asks him what he wants
                  to be when he grows up   *policeman*
soldier   at school   the teachers teach him to shoot
                      for the stars
                  to constellate
                        a body with bullets
              & baptize himself   white
                      in the light.

When people say, "we have made it through worse before"

Clint SMITH

all I hear is the wind slapping against the gravestones
of those who did not make it, those who did not
survive to see the confetti fall from the sky, those who

did not live to watch the parade roll down the street.
I have grown accustomed to a lifetime of aphorisms
meant to assuage my fears, pithy sayings meant to

convey that everything ends up fine in the end. There is no
solace in rearranging language to make a different word
tell the same lie. Sometimes the moral arc of the universe

does not bend in a direction that will comfort us.
Sometimes it bends in ways we don't expect & there are
people who fall off in the process. Please, dear reader,

do not say I am hopeless, I believe there is a better future
to fight for, I simply accept the possibility that I may not
live to see it. I have grown weary of telling myself lies

that I might one day begin to believe. We are not all left
standing after the war has ended. Some of us have
become ghosts by the time the dust has settled.

Moral Inventory

Ruth AWAD

What good is your goodness really,
if it is undone as soon as it begins?
I flew across an ocean slicked with plastic,
and I am still afraid of whales even though I know
they are choking on our trash.
I had money in my pocket from a job
of casual corporate-unkindness,
gave it to anyone who asked.
I want to be a better animal.
I want to love what I can while I can:
my dogs who cotton the grass,
a song that fills my cup and gallops me
under a hunter's moon. So what if I
snag in her antlers? I once had a body
that wasn't a body—it was a voice
in a god's mouth. It was the holy vowel.
Oh, animal, I thank you.
Oh, flank, oh, wanting gut,
say it matters, tell me to begin
again. Tell me, and I will.

Postcard from Gone

Leila CHATTI

When you left I walked
into the ocean. Not to
drown but to be held

by something
reluctant
to let go. Don't

make this bigger
than it is, which is big
enough to swallow

whales
and civilizations.
I joined

the blue, I was blue.
And when I looked
down, I shattered

and reformed
so many times, you know, I couldn't catch
a clear look at myself.

non-fiction

On Jellyfish

Nina Li COOMES

I. OCELLI

The first time I saw a beached jelly, it was on the wet-sand of the Japanese Pacific in winter. The eyeless jelly glistened on the sand, apathetic and opaque, slumped as if to say *dead or alive, who cares?* Can something with such a thin will be alive? A jellyfish washed up on a clouded beach reflects the gray and granite of both sand and sky. Its invertebrate, gut-less flop is a gelatinous shrug as if to render its own existence unimportant.

On bad days, I yearn to be a jellyfish. Half submerged in my cooling bath, I watch clouds pass in an ushering wind through the window. The water fills my open eyes. I imagine that I am reflecting the pink bath-bottom, the milk-blue sky. That I too am a fragile column, my body a glassy swimming pout. Something that is all outline and no substance. I linger, forcing my eyelids closed. The ropey tentacles of my hair curl and undulate around my face. I will them to nest around me. To pull my head gently from my neck. To swish water through the vessel of my skin. To sigh and sigh and sigh, propelled forward by each exhale. To be hollow. An underwater lantern, glowing a soft pink, neither existing or not existing, only passing through.

> Jellyfish are not fish, but we call them so. Death is not disappearing, but in these cushioned rooms, I call it so.

My ear cocoons the lulling tide of hushed breath. *Kietai*, I think. Incorrectly, I translate, *I want to die*. Later, fresh from my ineffectual therapy appointment, I will laugh bravely, gamely, teeth bared in a smiling grimace, chattering about how hard it is to translate the sentiment: kietai. To disappear, to wink out, to become something transparent, imbued in non-being, only observing, barely existing. You say this to an American therapist, and they cannot comprehend. English rushes us headlong into extremes. *Are you saying you want to die?* they ask. It is a puzzling question. What must I do to disappear? How do I say: *I do not want to die, but I do not want to exist*. Or *I am overwhelmed by jealousy for invertebrate zooplankton. For blind blossoms in water.* Jellyfish are not fish, but we call them so. Death is not disappearing, but in these cushioned rooms, I call it so. And so I settle for the next best approximation: *Yes, yes, the thing I am drifting toward, perhaps on purpose, perhaps not, is death. Yes, the thing I want is death. Yes, I suppose, if you say it that way, I want to die.*

Back in the bathtub, I think to myself again, *kietai*. Above me, the sun breaks through the frosted glass, a slow slice of light filtering through the watery bleak. I turn my face towards the column in unthinking motion. My eyes are briefly primordial, the multiple ocelli that dot the dome of a jelly fixating slowly towards something brighter. Flickering, patterned, rectangular cells of sun: an invitation to stay.

II. CNIDOCYTE

When I turned twenty-three, something strange began to happen to me. The natural anxieties of everyday life began to shift, twisting into shadows more sinister. I was used to small aches. I could handle my self-directed microaggressions. I could palm the brief spear of obsessive dislike at the spread of my thigh, the minute lurching doom of mortality inspired by a car scraping past me on the sidewalk. All this I could tolerate. But in February of my twenty-third year, I found myself completely hollow. I was invaded month after month by an emptiness that felt foreign and uncalled for. Half of the month, I was happy. Half of the month, I was in love. Half of the month, I woke up every day enamored by the automatic pull of the world on my body. And yet, for the other half of the month joy emptied out of me, leaving only a body yearning to disappear—why?

Of course, jellyfish are not simply beautiful manifestations of apathy. Some are very dangerous. Arguably the most dangerous of all jellyfish is the *Chironex fleckeri*. Sometimes known as the sea wasp, this highly venomous box jellyfish is utterly lovely and wholly lethal. It stretches ten feet of ghostly lace, its bell a transparent net of starry blue configurations. In water the sea wasp is nearly invisible. It drags a train of tentacles through the water, a treacherous bride dressed in venom. One box jellyfish is said to carry enough poison to kill sixty human adults. But the sea wasp is not a killing machine. It is discerning. Unlike other jellyfish, it has four clusters of twenty-four primordial eyes. It is capable of detecting light, perhaps even color. It does not drift, but hunts, propelling itself towards prey, refusing to rely on the nonchalant tangle of its cousins. Even its name, cheiro for the Greek word "hand" and nex for the Latin word meaning "murderer" is purposeful. *Chironex, hand-murderer*: the sea wasp will embrace you glove-like, tentacles zipping, a hand-picked death.

And yet—how strange—the venom of the *Chironex* is not even its own. In the tips of its tentacles live cnidocytes, dependent single cellular not-quite-organisms that pay bodily rent by existing as the *Chironex*'s stings. Without the cnidocytes, *Chironex* would simply be a box jellyfish of above-average intelligence. Its entire being has been colored by its foreign inhabitants' propensity for death.

The next year, I go to the doctor's office for an annual checkup. After the weighing and blood pressure checking, I lie back on the paper-covered surface and briefly gloss over the newly constant bi-weekly depression. *Probably just PMS*, I laugh. I am sure that wanting not to exist is simply part of what it means to exist in a woman's body. I tell the doctor, *Don't worry, it goes away as soon as my period comes*. The doctor shakes her head. She asks me to explain what I am enduring, this time with more detail. By the end of the appointment, she has given me a name for the darkness.

And at first, I am relieved. I indulge in a childhood ritual, stopping at a bakery for a freshly baked pita, creamy with labneh and zaatar. I am proud of myself for enduring the blood draws, the speculum, the scrape of the pap smear. I am a seven-year-old with a lollipop again. But then, I begin to read about my diagnosis. I read about a reality show star, her smile dense and saturated, who one day tangled herself in a noose. I read of women relegated to taking drugs that cause cysts to break deep and wide across their faces, their bodies swelling beyond recognition, expanding and contracting with fluid. I read of women who weep and laugh in terrifying syncopation. I read the reports of medical professionals who say no such diagnosis exists—that it is a culture-bound phenomena, and I wonder to myself what they mean. Culture-bound, as in our culture causes this toxicity to well in our bodies so we cannot help but become poisonous? Culture-bound, as in I can recognize the depression now and call it by name, but still, there is no guarantee it will abate? Culture-bound, as in body-bound, as in the wanton trail of the cnidocyte? The bind of a hand named Murder, though it has no choice in being such? As if we cannot escape the skin or space we are in, no matter how much we wish to empty ourselves of it?

III. NERVE NET

I want to stay.

I will say it again: I want to stay.

I want to stay. And that is why I do not let myself think of the specifics of the darkness, though I have been given its name.

    Instead I abstract it, comparing myself to an invertebrate to cope. I watch the lopsided frill of a nettle jelly, a field of waning clovers decorating the moon jellyfish. I think of their primitive eyes, their stings, their general lack of a central nervous system, relying instead on a nerve net, neurons scattershot like constellations through their forms, feeling everything at once, but nothing specifically. I imagine the nudge of water against a body of film. I imagine spores of sun puncturing a jelly's bell. I imagine unfurling my own nerve net.

    Consider: the funky salt of shoyu poured into an avocado's verdant hollow; the pink-tiled bathroom and its window of clouds; the percussion of the elevated train at night; the Gauguin palette of open air vegetable markets in Queens; the smell of warm dirt; the smell of new morning; the feeling of good cinema, how it pushes your heart just slightly wider; your adult sister still wanting to lie in a pile with you on winter afternoons; kerosene stoves; friend-dates; regular dates; last night you turned to your lover and said *Make me forget all of this* and he did; and later, weeping into his gray waffle-knit shirt; my friends, their laughter slack jawed and honking across the table at; Big Wong; swimming in Lake Michigan at night; the voice of friends now piped through the radio; butter on thick-cut toast; white rice and oily seaweed; the hiss of the radiator; a hymn out of vogue; wood burning; the way summer sidles up flirtatiously and suddenly you are bare-armed and dancing; walking home; your mother; mama; the slow swivel of your faces towards the light; every morning your father prays *Thank you God, for fresh air and blue sky*; a preponderance of evidence; a totality flush against your skin; everything specifically and nothing at all; a command; an invitation; a prayer; *Stay*.

Yesterday Is a Wild Parrot

David ROMPF

One morning several months after his heart surgery, my father says, "I'm surprised the bears didn't get into the trash last night." He's dipping sweet cinnamon toast into coffee, which has been his breakfast every day since coming home from the hospital. The toast is crisp, more cracker than bread, each piece the size of an index card. He ate this same hard toast as a child in Michigan. He claims it tastes exactly as it did nearly eighty years ago.

"I don't think there have been any bears here for awhile," I tell him. I'm sitting on a folding chair next to the hospital bed we've installed for my father in the den. Every day during visits from New York, I drink my first cup of coffee with him, and we talk. "But I saw a raccoon the other night. He took his time as he crossed the street as if he ruled the neighborhood."

"They can be mean," he says. "I don't like raccoons."

It's Monday, trash pick-up day in our southern California county named for orange groves long since replaced by housing tracts and strip malls. A possum has been seen scurrying around the neighborhood on the cinderblock fences separating one home from another. Occasionally the raccoon shows up, evicting two stray cats who have become regular backyard squatters. A lone rat often drills across the telephone wires, always in the same direction, east to west, and always in the minutes after sunset. All forms of life, imaginary and otherwise, seem to thrive around us. One day I go outside, stand on the lawn, and scan all the trees within view. Years ago, flocks of wild parrots began swooping down from the sky, pausing en masse on the magnolias. Their appearance was sudden, erratic, without precedent. No one knew where the birds came from—perhaps Mexico or Central America. Their raucous fugue seemed a demonic possession. They squawked and flew from tree to tree, and then they were gone. I had not seen those parrots in many years, but I look for them now.

Our suburban menagerie is varied, but if there were bears here, they moved away centuries ago. The nearest wild bear lives a hundred miles to the north-east, five thousand feet up in the mountains where, on two or three long-ago winter weekends, my father drove up a winding incline so my sister and I could ride plastic toboggans in the snow.

My father's bear, at first, seems to come out of nowhere, the idea of it held over from a lingering dream, or perhaps a result of too much staring at the stucco ceiling in the den, where he will stay for who knows how long—until he can walk again and take showers again and prepare his own soup for lunch, or maybe forever. Fierce infections had kept him quarantined in the hospital for months, causing his muscles to atrophy. Now he spends all his time in a wheelchair at the kitchen table or in his bed. As we talk over coffee, I soon realize he might be blending memories of his youth in Michigan with those of his life in California. I wonder if the taste of cinnamon toast has helped him merge these two realms into a continuum of reality with rearranged plots.

For entertainment on summer evenings in Michigan's Upper Peninsula people drove to the public dump and waited for the black bears. The animals would waddle out of the woods and across mounds of garbage, ripping open paper bags and milk cartons stuffed with edible scraps. This was fishing country. Trout heads and perch bones were prime, but the bears also relished the stale bread that had been tossed around the dump to lure them into the open. As soon as my father mentioned the bear, I remembered the summer we returned to Michigan and, for a day, we drove deep into a forest on a road that no one travels any more, a work camp route from the early 1900s. When the road ended, we proceeded on a grown-over gravel trail, the underbrush scraping beneath the car. In the fly-buzzing heat, we looked for deer and bear, not to hunt but to observe. I had never seen a bear in the wild. That day we spotted a black bear and thirteen deer, some of them mothers with spring fawns. In the distance, the bear seemed small, barely larger than a child's toy; it was nothing like the grizzlies I had seen on television and thus imagined finding in the wild. Resting on its hindquarters, rocking slightly, it nibbled field grass and berries, seemingly oblivious to our intrusion into the center of its world.

In the evening, my father asks me if I am going to sleep upstairs. This house he and my mother have lived in since moving west, the one I grew up in, has three bedrooms but only one story. I don't know what house he's thinking about: perhaps his childhood home in Houghton, Michigan, or one of the upper-level apartments my parents rented after I was born but before they moved west.

"I'm sleeping in Patti's room," I say.

"Oh," he says, but I can see that he's flummoxed. He wonders whether my sister's room is located upstairs in the house that I now perceive as several homes melded in his mind, places from his past and the house in which we ponder bears straying from the distant woods of memory.

In the morning, he still asks, "Did you sleep well upstairs?"

I would come to like this idea of an imagined upstairs bedroom where I could read myself to sleep, removed from the endless routines of caregiving and the clamor of television game shows. My father's figment created a space elevated, in my own imagination, beyond the reach of illness and suffering, if only for a time. His reinvention of our house, its dreamlike expansion, offered a paradox: the room upstairs was anchored in our home, and in the joy and struggle embodied by it, while also hovering afloat as a placid mystery. In the evenings, on my way to bed, I began to walk down the hallway as if ascending stairs to an attic or climbing a ladder to a serene treehouse. The room became a fantasy I gladly elected to enter.

I began saying to my father, "Goodnight, Dad. I'm going upstairs now."

"Okay," he said. "Sleep well."

His hallucinations first began in the hospital. Until the surgery, my father's mind was sharper than his butcher's knives, his power of recall formidable. He could recite the long serial number of his army rifle issued sixty years ago. He subscribed to three newspapers and retained prodigious amounts of information. He had shown no signs of waning memory. His parents, who lived into their mid-eighties, maintained their cognitive ability until the end. On my mother's side of the family, a different story: several of her aunts had Alzheimer's or other forms of dementia; her own mother probably would have followed the pattern had she not died from lung cancer.

> I would come to like this idea of an imagined upstairs bedroom where I could read myself to sleep, removed from the endless routines of caregiving and the clamor of television game shows.

In the hospital one morning, as we stood beside his bed, my father said, "I saw ants crawling around the clock, and other animals too." He had cats and dogs as a child. Old pictures show him grinning with kittens piled in his lap, so it was not surprising that creatures of all kinds figured prominently in his fabulist creations at home and on the critical care unit. Spiders swarmed the ceiling, a giraffe came to greet him, and children gleefully chased each other around his room.

One night at the hospital, long past visiting hours, a bevy of nuns came to see him.

"I'm going to complain to the diocese," he said. He didn't want nuns anywhere near him, especially when he was supposed to be sleeping.

He never seemed to mind the animals, though.

In the mornings, he often woke up thinking he was on a ship. On the way to his army post in Austria, my father had crossed the Atlantic on a naval vessel, where he slept in a twelfth deck bunk. It was his first grand adventure in life, the ocean a bracing surge into the future. His job was to cook breakfast, lunch, and dinner for his shipmates, ever-hungry men from every part of America. In the hospital, he worried whether there was enough food for his current voyage.

"I hope we'll make it," he said.

On other days he believed he was on a train destined for cities we visited on a family trip to Europe after my year abroad in London. "We had a good trip to Belgium," he said, but we had never been to Belgium. I looked around his hospital room. His bed was next to a wall of large windows overlooking a neighborhood lush with palm, jacaranda, and juniper trees. It was easy to understand how he envisioned a passing countryside. Outside his room, nurses and doctors walked to and fro, carrying on with their duties. They could be crew or fellow passengers on board a train or a ship to anywhere, or everywhere. Suddenly I saw the orderlies who mopped the floors as deckhands, and the blinking, humming hospital machines as instruments keeping our vessel on its intended path.

One evening, a nurse new to my father's care asked him what he had done for a living before his retirement.

"You'll laugh when I tell you," he said.

"I won't laugh," she said. "I promise."

"I was in the circus."

"And what did you do in the circus?" the kind nurse asked.

"I was the boss!"

He had never been in the circus. After his stint as an army cook, he worked in supermarkets for more than thirty-five years as a meat cutter, and never as boss.

The animal kingdom in his room and the journeys over land and sea persisted during the months spent in two hospitals and a nursing facility. After the giraffes and nuns first visited, we mentioned my father's visions to a nurse.

"Oh, it's probably sundowners," she said. None of us had ever heard the term. The nurse left the room without elaborating, so I did some research and learned that sundowners syndrome—or "sundowning"—can affect people with dementia and elderly patients recovering from surgery. The common symptom is an onset of confusion in the late afternoon and early evening. "The changing light and the shadows can trigger it," another nurse explained. Morphine also causes hallucinations, but the drug hadn't been given to my father.

In the hospital and nursing home, his memory loss and confusion became protracted, starting before late afternoon and continuing long past sundown. At home, his long journeys by train and by sea continued, with a cast of ever-changing characters joining him along the way. Sometimes he thought my sister was my niece or that I was a doctor. He could not remember what year it was or the name of the president. On my birthday, eight months after his surgery, he thought I was turning seventy-five.

"But you look good for your age," he said.

"Dad, if I'm turning seventy-five, how old is Mom?"

"Ninety-two," he said. "But she's not looking too good."

> We laugh when my father gets our ages wrong, and he laughs too when we correct him. After a while, it's not clear when he's forgetting or pretending.

My mother, just five days earlier, had turned seventy-four. When they first met at the A&P where he was cutting meat in the late 1950s, she was sixteen, my father a scandalous twenty-five. Soon he would be taking her and her younger sisters out for rides in his Chevy, or they would go downtown to watch a movie. He remembers calling my mother by an affectionate nickname, *Killer*, which infuriated her father but apparently captivated her. One afternoon my mother locked herself in the bathroom. From behind the closed door, she said she wouldn't come out until her parents agreed to let her marry the butcher. They insisted she wait until after she finished high school and turned eighteen. A deal was struck, and they were married three months after her threshold birthday.

We laugh when my father gets our ages wrong, and he laughs too when we correct him. After a while, it's not clear when he's forgetting or pretending. Our displeasure with being twenty years older than we are provides new entertainment for him.

Although he never forgets his birthdate or the precise day of his inscription into the army, sometimes he adds or subtracts ten years from his age and waits for our reaction.

Occasionally he also gives me an extra sister.

"What's your other sister's name?" he asks one morning as we drink our coffee.

"I have only one sister, Dad."

"Oh."

"Patti."

"Right. You're sure?"

"Yes. Just one."

I don't know if he's confused or if he's pulling my leg, testing my patience and aiming for a reaction. Could his miscount be traced to having two sisters of his own, or to my mother's two sisters? Someone has two sisters around here, his expression seems to say, and maybe they live in the room upstairs.

For now, my father's mixed-up memories lead me happily astray, his confusion serving as an unexpected buffer between my relative youth and old age. With our lifetimes in constant flux, the future seems elastic, stretched indefinitely before us. However warped or misleading the illusion, as long as my father is alive, I will be young, regardless of my real or imagined age. After major surgery and savage infections, after processions of animals and dreamlike landscapes, my father has prevailed. Grappling with my own mortality, I hitch my hope to this man. I see him as proof that humans can withstand unimaginable trauma, and that life can be long despite grueling setbacks.

But then there are periods of true blankness, as on the morning my mother and I sit beside him at the kitchen table.

"When's David coming?" my father asks, looking only at my mother.

I do not speak or move. Among his plunges into absolute confusion, this one strips me of all defenses. If I was not David sitting next to him, who was I? Perhaps wrongly, I assume he has registered my presence but not my identity. Yet maybe my very presence eludes him too, for he has not asked my mother about the man sitting next to him—me, his only son. He has not asked whether the man has a name or why he is here. He has not looked me in the eyes. In this moment of being and not being, of missing my identity as his son, I feel like the personification of the room upstairs or the mythic animals prowling our neighborhood.

I cannot bring myself to answer: I'm already here, Dad.

Instead, my mother says, "He's here!"

She glances at me with an expression that means: give him a minute, he's just tired and confused.

"Oh," my father says.

He turns to me and studies my face. I can detect his attempt to seize the present, accurate reality, if such a thing exists, and to remember that I have been here next to him all along.

"Dad, it's me," I say. "I came home yesterday."

"It's nice to have you here again," he says. "I missed you."

One moment I was invisible or unknown, and then, like the wild parrots, I have returned.

My Sometimes Vietnamese

An UONG

I don't think I have a personality in Vietnamese anymore, though I'm not convinced I ever did. There's a way of sharing laughter and sadness in the language that escapes me. My Vietnamese is a limited arsenal of phrases and words communicated with fluency but not with intimacy. Speaking it is an act of contortion—one in which my body knows the shape but not how to become it. The tenderness it once held is buried deep in my childhood memories, ones of my mother telling me family stories, or of my father singing in the shower.

There is too much calculation now. Too much of a pause between thought and speech when I try to splice together pieces of a language I use dutifully to tell my mother I love her and to tell my father to be safe. It is something I pull from awkwardly at family gatherings in America to address my aunts and uncles with respect, yet there is little of it to turn to when my cousins in Vietnam try to joke with me. The words once lived in a small apartment in Los Angeles shared by myself, my little brother, and my parents—but not much elsewhere. Families who shared our language were few and far between in our neighborhood, and the closest Vietnamese community was at least a three-hour bus ride away.

For some time after my family settled in America, my mother would do my elementary school homework with me. We were both starting from the bottom, she at thirty-five and myself at four. There was little to guide us beyond the colorful picture books that we borrowed from the library. Together we learned the curves and edges of English words. They came to shape the world we entered as strangers; the giant metal boxes on wheels we knew as *xe hơi* gained a new identity as car. The room in our apartment where my mother cooked aromatic dinners transformed from *bếp* to kitchen.

Vietnamese is a language that dances when it wants to and cuts when it has to. The words come forth from the back of the mouth and must be formed with care. In a language where *xe* and *xé* have very different meanings because accent marks dictate whether one's tone should rise, dip or curve, the tongue has to navigate lithely.

The assignments from that time required repetition, and we would take turns practicing our letters and words. One afternoon I held my head in my small hands as the pairing of word to meaning escaped me. Learning a new language was learning a new life, and I didn't know how to leap over that chasm. My mother sat next to me while my brother napped, floating dust caught in a ray of sunlight above his head.

"I can't do this," I said to my mom. "I don't know this

word." It was *tower*, and I could not in my mind imagine its real-life contours, the absoluteness of brick and stone rising toward cloudless sky. My mother could not point to its meaning either. I pushed my papers away and looked at her with wet eyes.

"Are you doing homework for you, or are you doing it for me?" she asked. Her Vietnamese is precise and cutting when she's upset. She wields it in a way she will never wield English, yet to argue with her in Vietnamese is to be talked in circles toward inevitable defeat. Her dark eyes lingered on me, then she turned away, to check on my brother.

"For you," I said. "It's for you."

"No. It's for yourself!" my mother snapped, head turning back so quickly that her short ponytail swung from side to side. "Why would it be for me? It's for your future."

I didn't understand why she was so upset. I was learning English to serve my parents, where they were not able to serve themselves. At the bank, the grocery store, the pharmacy—I was the little girl with the quivering voice standing between them and every counter in town. I didn't know it at the time, but my mother didn't want that to be the case. She needed it, but she didn't want it. My mother was ashamed of not being able to help her own daughter, and what was previously unspoken splayed itself before us in my confession that day.

I surpassed my mother in English as my schooling continued, and she fell back without resources to grow the knowledge she did have. I lived two lives throughout my years in school, returning home to a place where my words occupied a separate universe, one in which I bowed my head toward aunts and uncles at family gatherings, always making sure I addressed them correctly. A small slip could result in offense.

This is the same universe where my mother told us ghost

stories during afternoons spent sitting by the front door, watching my father prepare for work. She told us of the girl who was bewitched by a spirit at the graveyard, and of the soldiers who bought cursed vegetables from streetside ghosts. During these hours leading up to sunset, Vietnamese held the warmth of my mother's ringing laughter, a laugh that tilted her head back and shook her shoulders. In this world perched on the edge of our front door, Vietnamese was not something I was ashamed to speak.

The shift went in both directions; as I learned the ways of American English, I began to lose my Vietnamese, a language my mother holds so close that she whispers it in her sleep. "What's the word for..." I started to say more often to her as I patch-worked together a meaning close to what I wanted. "Viện bảo tàng," she said to me once when I asked for the Vietnamese equivalent of museum, except I said to her, "the word that means the place you visit to look at paintings."

With that change came a loss of intimacy. Even in the most heated moments with my mother, I could never speak to her with agency and confidence, always leaving our arguments wishing they had taken place in English instead.

"What? What?" my mother would say to me as I stumbled through my words, trying to compete against her in Vietnamese.

Out there—in grocery stores, by bus stops, at school events—my mother's Vietnamese made my stomach coil with the heat of embarrassment. Her loudness turned too many heads, quieted too many surrounding conversations. My teen-aged self saw our neighbors eyeing her with a condescension she was too boisterous to notice herself. While Vietnamese kept her from assimilating in America, English gave me a control I could use to shape my own life.

Dạ, pronounced "ya" with a descending tone, was always the word used most often with my parents. It means "yes," but in a way that requires a slight bow of the head toward my mother and father, a quiet suppression of any disagreement that might exist. Throughout my childhood, I said it so often that aunts and uncles thought I could say nothing else. My English-soaked adolescence taught me the finite power of "no," of shaking my head in a way I wasn't allowed to with my family. In Vietnamese, I was dutiful. Never funny, never sassy. I've always wondered: How much of this was part of my personal identity as a soft-spoken human, and how much of it came from a lifetime of learning that as a young woman in Vietnamese culture, I had to follow social hierarchies woven together long before I was born?

In this world perched on the edge of our front door, Vietnamese was not something I was ashamed to speak.

My cousins in Vietnam spoke with quick exchanges that bounced from person to person, usually ending in a communal laughter I could only pretend to share. The one time I visited as a teenager, we sat on the black and white linoleum floor of my mother's childhood home, and my cousins asked me to repeat certain words in Vietnamese, ones they knew sounded funny coming from my unsure mouth. It was strange, they said, the way that my accent curved the wrong way sometimes, washing away the steep dip or slight twirl that was supposed to accompany those phrases.

Years later, during a stroll through the Milwaukee Art Museum, I approached a gallery docent to ask for a map of the building. "May I perchance have a map?" I asked her. There was a pause. A blink of her long-lashed blue eyes. Blond strands shifted on her shoulders as she turned to look at me. She scanned my face: Tan skin, straight black hair, eyes most passersby would label as "almond-shaped." Maybe she wouldn't have been able to pinpoint it exactly to Vietnamese, but by every measure of appearance, I am undeniably Asian. And apparently, that's all she saw of me.

The docent finally responded, "I only have them in English here. Is that okay?"

I said yes and took the pamphlet, but wandered through the rest of the exhibits in a daze. I worked so hard, I thought to myself. *Too hard to be asked if English is okay*. Halfway through an undergraduate education at the time, I buried myself in 18th Century literature while slowly forgetting Vietnamese words I was once able to pull out smoothly.

When I left home for college in New York, the silence left by lack of Vietnamese was filled with conversations among friends and classmates from all over the world. I drank their words and only spoke Vietnamese when my mother called once a week. Sometimes, I caught Vietnamese on the subway, in the Manhattan crowds, or at Asian grocery stores. Most times I walked on, pretending not to hear, and other times I stood still and listened, soaking in every lilt and curl, admitting to myself a homesickness for a language I too often took for granted when I was younger.

Once, at a gift shop in Manhattan's Chinatown, the owner looked at me and just knew. "Cháu muốn cái nào?" she asked me as I looked at her collection of rings, my nose inches away from the countertop. *Which one would you like?* "I'm sorry?" I responded in English instinctively, taken aback by her recognition and confidence. She looked a bit older than my mother, with similar wrinkles near her eyes and the same graying hair falling above her shoulders. Her smile faded slightly.

"Sorry, sorry," she said in English, then picked up her newspaper.

I could have reached out in Vietnamese. Instead, I walked away with a mix of guilt and sadness in my chest, knowing that she was looking for a moment of community and that my Vietnamese was too cold for bantering. "Yes, ma'am," I would have replied. "Thank you, ma'am," I would have continued, and "goodbye ma'am," I would have said eventually. It didn't matter that I knew more words than that. It mattered that I would not have known how to use them.

Vietnamese is a language both integral and strange to me. It is integral in the way that it roots me to a calendar of my family's cultural rituals, each holding the same magic from my mother's afternoon ghost stories. Every late January or early February, firecrackers bursts into gray swirls along the streets. "Chúc mừng năm mới!" I say to my parents over the phone. *Happy New Year.* By the time April arrives with the anniversary of Saigon's fall in 1975, my thoughts are caught in my mother's stories—tales of not seeing her own father for months at a time. "Xin lỗi," I say as I hear her voice lower during our call. *I'm sorry.* September brings with it the chill of a fiery sunset, followed by a glowing moon above treetops. "Chúc mừng trung thu," I say to my parents' pixelated faces on the computer screen as we video chat. *Happy Mid-Autumn Festival.* They wish me the same as they hold up their mooncakes, already cut into fourths to share.

I held Vietnamese at arm's length in my adolescence, but the distance between myself and the home where I have spoken it most has reminded me to become reacquainted with it. In the Vietnamese community where I work today, the language is shared between high school students walking home from school or middle-aged men sipping coffees. Their conversations remind me of my cousins in Vietnam, and the summer in high school spent deciphering their inside jokes.

During my first week in the neighborhood, I visited a nearby Vietnamese bakery with hopes of breaking away from my tongue-tying nerves. As I approached Chau's Bakery, I practiced my order: "Dạ, cho con một ổ bánh mì." I repeated it to myself as my feet carried me toward the store's yellow awning. *Please, may I have a sandwich. Please, may I have a sandwich.*

Inside, the pressed tin ceiling hovered high above the display case and kitchen beyond. Foot-long French loaves were stacked behind glass, and the enveloping smell of baking bread held a warmth to it. To the left of the entrance, a refrigerator with a glass door housed containers of pickled leeks, sausages wrapped in banana leaves, and packages of tofu. I pretended to scan these items as I tried to figure out how I should address the cashier.

She didn't look older than sixty, which meant I couldn't call her bác—*older aunt*—for risk of insulting her age, but the lines under her cheekbones and slight wrinkles at the edges of her eyes ruled out the use of chị—*sister*—which would be disrespectful. I settled for cô—*slightly older aunt*.

"Chào cô," I said to her. *Hello, (slightly older) aunt.* A moment of hesitation, then: "Dạ, cho con một ổ bánh mì." I asked for the sandwich, but it feels alien to speak Vietnamese with a stranger.

"Thịt nguội hay thịt nướng?" she asked, a little too quickly. *Cold meat or barbecued beef?*

I was not prepared for this question, a disruption to the script in my head. I was also not prepared for her thick northern Vietnamese accent, which bent her words into tones I never heard in my southern Vietnamese household.

"Thịt nguội hay thịt nướng?" She repeated the question with an emphasis on each word.

"Thịt nướng," I said. As she began to put my sandwich together, I tried to think of questions to ask her. *How long have you been here? What region of northern Vietnam are you from?* Anything to replicate the small talk I heard elsewhere in the neighborhood. Somewhere between my brain and my mouth, the words stalled themselves.

A customer came into the store with a list of requests before I was able to say anything else. Recognition of familiarity between the two women was instantaneous; a back-and-forth followed, one in which they traded family stories and recent life developments. By the time my sandwich was done, their words were moving with such speed that it became difficult for me to cling onto the meaning of their sentences.

I paid, whispered "Thank you" and walked away. As I left the bakery, the two women continued their banter. One laughed loudly, high-pitched, and staggered. My Vietnamese existed in this way, somewhere outside of their world. Disjointed by a childhood of isolated use geared toward respect and duty, it floated around as I tried to anchor it in my being.

FICTION

Eucharist

Patricia PATTERSON

The night of Ernesto's death, Sandra shuts off all the lights in her home and sits at the kitchen table, breaking off pieces of tostada. She makes a ritual of it, splitting apart bits of maize, suppressing thoughts of her brother's spirit drifting into the afterlife. Sandra imagines Ernesto there: confused, flailing in empty space. Alone. She snaps the first tostada into jagged pieces. Sandra sets a sliver in her mouth, the texture brittle between her teeth.

The cuckoo clock strikes every half hour, the bird's shrill laughter, harsh against the quiet room, and every half hour Sandra crosses herself and whispers into the dark: "En el nombre del Padre, y del Hijo, y del Espíritu Santo. Amen." Then she follows the Blessed Sacrament. She separates the second tostada into three sections, sharp with edges like canine teeth. *El Padre, el Hijo, y el Espíritu Santo.* She scatters the broken bread on her raw cedar table: uneven pieces severed from the body. Another tostada. Three. Sandra swallows; shards like splintered glass catching the roof of her mouth. She breaks the suffering, parts the flesh.

Another half-hour: the bird in the clock springs and Sandra breaks the body again. The bird sounds different every time it wakes. Sandra falls into sync with the bird. The bird springs. Sandra breaks. She eats. The bird springs. She breaks. She eats again. When Mamá calls, Sandra sits at her kitchen table, trying to block out the echoes of the rings. Mamá leaves no voicemail. Sandra prays words she can no longer taste. Prayers spin around her brain like a carousel. Throughout the night, Sandra consumes pounds of corn and meat and sangre. She stops at twelve tostadas, not knowing why she stops or if she even wants to stop. Part of her feels she can go on living this way.

The clock hands twitch into early morning. Sandra saves two tostadas for Ernesto's spirit and lays meat out to dry on the windowsill. She slices too much aguacate, spills black beans on the stovetop. She makes an altar of her kitchen.

Ernesto had been the kind of older brother that drank too much and ate too little. In life, he had gambled often, wasting money on things he didn't need, like neon lights for his pickup truck and dozens of designer shoes that fit loose around his ankles. Perhaps he had cared too little about his future, but he had always been good to Sandra, his only sister, the only person whose future mattered. When Sandra had debated about going to college, Ernesto had said, "Don't give up on school. You're too fucking smart to end up working some bullshit job like me." Then when she said nothing in return, he whispered, "Christo, Sandra!"

Ernesto was never bothered by vulgarities, like using the

Lord's name in vain, and this had bothered Sandra. But she had never thought to question his faith. Ernesto had always been honest; this revealed a sense of morality. God would have forgiven him if there had been a little more time. Perhaps this is why Sandra now abandons tostadas on the dining room table. What if she can love her brother into salvation, enough to send him to a better resting place? "Padre," Sandra whispers, "grant his spirit safe passage to Heaven." She doesn't add, "Take me instead" or, "Sorry for the unorthodox shrine. It's not really for you."

Mamá calls again. It must be an unkindly hour in the morning because the rings echo a little deeper and feel even more abrasive, bouncing off the empty corners of the kitchen. Sandra tunes out the click of the hands on the clock and forgets that clocks can do such a thing as count down to another tomorrow. She forgets how to get up from a chair, to find her bed, to sleep a little. Mamá must sense her forgetting. This time she leaves a voicemail.

Sandra doesn't stir to check the message, but she figures it's probably something loud as voicemails from Mamá usually are. Something seemingly gentle like, "¿Mijita, donde andas? Call me back." Just more accusatory in tone, the way Mamá's Spanish makes Sandra feel like she has done something she should be ashamed of. Like all the times Mamá says, "I'm just worried about you," but instead it sounds like she's angry with Sandra. Mamá's words feel like contradictions; like bitter truths wrapped in kindness. Like she really means to say, "Damn it, Sandra! Me das un dolor de cabeza con tus tonterías." Like, "Don't fucking bother me with your stupid shit, Sandra. You'll give me a heart attack. And I damn near expect to live 'til I'm ninety-eight." Except, in Sandra's mind, everything is in Spanish, and it's all too fast, all too loud. Too much Mamá to handle. Especially when Sandra can't even get up from her kitchen table.

Sometimes Sandra imagines what Mamá was like before her birth. She imagines Mamá with an unfamiliar lightness: her hair long and loose over her shoulders, her smile shifting her features into different shapes, her eyes softer. She thinks Mamá would be different if Papá had never left; she often wonders where he went. She wonders why he abandoned a six-year-old Ernesto and Mamá, pregnant with Sandra, in Wasco—a space nestled between all the Santas and Sans of California, a plain so flat and un-saintly—and drifted to a place unknown. Most days, Sandra likes to pretend she knows where she could find him. She imagines Papá blending into the hilly streets of San Miguel de Allende and all the colorful adobe homes and soft tortillas and street vendors who yell, "¡Tamales Oaxaqueños!" to closed doors, windows cracked slightly to welcome in daylight, while everyone sleeps or nibbles on conchas and bolillos because it's just too early for shouts and savory foods. Here, the street vendors don't care about waking the roosters, much less the townsfolk, as they roll their carts with elote con chile and paletas over cobblestone, their wheels loose and their utensils clinking against metal.

Sandra knows little about Papá, but she knows one thing for sure: Papá left with a woman who was not Mamá, and Mamá didn't want to talk about it. Not ever. Sandra can never ask about Papá without Mamá saying something like, "Why do you want to know about that asshole? ¡Nos abandonó! You hear me? He is no man to me." Sandra often wonders what her parents had looked like when they were in love or if it had all just been a fairytale.

Then Sandra would say something like, "Pero Mamí, ¿donde vive ahora?"

And Ernesto would butt in with his smart mouth, breaking

up the Spanish like he always did, just for the sake of rebellion. "I hope he gets fucked by a fish," he would say. "¡Que le folle un pez!" And Sandra would sit with that awful obscenity, wondering why Ernesto found crass jokes so funny and wondering why Mamá and Ernesto always skirted around her question—where is Papá now?

Sandra leaves the unleavened bread on the table. For the next three days, she eats standing up and only when she has to. Only when her bones creak in that muted tune that might suggest she needs more calcium or more bones. Only when she notices her skin: taut across her cheekbones and sternum. In moments like these, Sandra remembers that her flesh is a dress for her bones. Mamá would curse at her if she saw her in such a state.

"¡Siéntate, flaca!" she would say. "Sit down. What are you? A maid?" Then Mamá would spoon feed her rice and black beans as if she were trying to break the surface of the earth with a shovel.

As the tostadas sit in the dry heat of her home, flies accumulate and roast. Die in a shrine of meat. *Mijita*, Mamá texts, *I'm coming.*

It's the thunder that wakes Sandra. She looks up at the cuckoo clock. 6:15. No bird. She stirs in a state of simultaneous worry and confusion, her body stiffening against the wall by the front door. Her legs wobble as she stands. She can't remember why she decided to sit here, by the curtains and the shoe rack and the doorbell, and when did she doze off? Did she go to work in the morning? 6:17. She remembers. Mamá is on her way. 6:18. She knows Mamá will be here soon; the thunder warns her, rattles the house with its low grumbling. 6:20. The kitchen. Sandra remembers the kitchen. The tostadas. The meat. The flies.

Mamá will be disturbed by the mess. Mamá will scold her. Sandra must sweep, must clear the house of the remains. Must clear the house of the smell. She thinks of Ernesto. She can't remember if it had been raining three nights ago, the night she learned he was dead, but she feels it must have been raining, the kind of rain accompanied by thunder so forceful it threatened to rattle the rooftops. The kind where lightning splits trees in half.

6:30. The bird returns. It bops its head downward, pecking at empty air. "Cuckoo," Sandra whispers to her little friend. *Cuckoo.* The bird mimics Sandra. She smiles. It returns to its hole in the clock, a safe burrow. Sandra turns on the television. It takes a moment for the screen to settle into color. The news is still on. Sandra has kept the television on the same channel for days, half-expecting to see Ernesto's face every time, knowing this is as irrational as the shrine in her kitchen. Sandra knows Ernesto isn't worth the pixelated space on the screen. His death means nothing to the town of Wasco. Headlines flash across the bottom of the screen: "Father of two killed after falling from taxi window onto busy motorway" ... "Despite warnings, FDA approves opioid painkillers" ... "Mario Segale, the inspiration for Nintendo's Hero Plumber, has died." She reads these with mild disinterest.

Sandra's mind whirls with alternate endings. He was in a car. He was out of a car. His girlfriend Christie was there. He hit a deer. He hit a tree. Someone hit him. It was a head-on collision. It was a murder. Her brother had jumped off a bridge. He was just going for a swim; he said he wouldn't be long. No, he wasn't on the road at all. He was in the barn behind Christie's father's house. A horse kicked him in the face. He had a stroke. He was so young. His body was found elsewhere. His cigarette cast hay into flames. Up he went with the smoke. Christie's father hit him over the head with an empty liquor bottle. Christie caught him cheating. She slit his throat. He bled out in the river by the state line. How did he get there? Where was his body? He was still alive. It was just a prank.

Sandra can't remember who called first or what was said exactly. But she knew before she picked up. She knew the moment the phone rang, and the person on the other side of the line took a moment too long to whisper, "Sandra?" She listened with ears that no longer belonged to her. When someone dies like that, words shift like clockwork. Sandra lived five hours in two minutes. Then everyone knew. She didn't have to tell them. The hours had already shifted the world into a state of knowing. Who picked up the phone first? Who thought to call the next person? Sandra wishes Ernesto died a hero's death, brave and stupid, an ending that would give his life meaning. Not this. Not this mistake. Sandra would rather spend her time imagining a different reality where her brother hadn't gone this way, at thirty-two, barely an adult. Ernesto decided this fate. And he didn't stop to think about all the shit he would leave behind: pieces of garbage that Sandra and Mamá would have to box and throw out later, all the hours' worth of packing and deliberating, all the damn mail they would have to sort and return to sender. And, worst of all, he never fucking thought of Sandra. How he would leave her to wait on Mamá. That rampant knock on her door. The echoes of Mamá's voice: "Sandra, ¿estas ahí?" How she would never have the guts to say, "No, Mamá. I'm not here" like Ernesto. Ernesto had gusto. Sandra had liked that about him. He would scream, "¡Ay, caray, Mamá! Stay out of my business." Then he would crack open a bottle of Corona, wedge a lime in, and ignore her shadow skulking at the door.

83

Mamá starts with the kitchen. She sweeps, scrubs the floors with a brittle-sounding brush, soaks the counters in vinegar, and opens the windows and the back door. "Mugre moscas," she says to the flies, turning her back to Sandra. "¡Pinche malvados!" She swats them with her shoe, chasing one around the kitchen until it collapses from fear, and collects the dead ones in a dustpan. She avoids eye contact and curses the flies some more. Sandra lets her roam the space like a wild boar. For once, the flies are to blame, not Sandra.

"He loved you," Mamá says, neglecting her Spanish the way Ernesto used to. Perhaps this is her way of honoring his memory. "Before you were born, he told me he wanted a baby sister. He said, 'If it's not a girl, don't come home.'" Mamá laughs. "¡Que terco era! So headstrong, even as a child."

Ernesto was brilliant, but he was constantly dumbing himself down. He worked a construction job, not because it was something he had to do or something he wanted to do, but because it was precisely the kind of job where he wasn't expected to do anything beyond a given project. He welcomed the static. There were no surprises.

Once, when Sandra was eleven years old, she asked him why he was flunking chemistry. Mamá had already chided him about his report card, and Sandra had listened in the doorway of the kitchen. Everything important in their lives seemed to happen in the kitchen. "You like science," Sandra said. "It doesn't make sense why you would make such bad grades." Sandra had often watched Ernesto in their backyard, filling empty soda bottles with ingredients and waiting for chemical reactions. He seemed to always know what he was doing and wore rubber gloves that were so long they covered the skin above his elbows. To this, he shrugged and said, "So, I like to blow shit up. That doesn't make me smart."

Mamá is no longer cleaning, no longer shifting across space like a vacuum. There's a silence about her that unsettles Sandra. She doesn't ask Sandra what led her to this ceremony in the first place: why the meat was scattered on the windowsill; why all the lights were off until Mamá turned them on; why there were small shards of tostada scattered on the kitchen table and across the linoleum floors. She doesn't ask Sandra about God, either, but Sandra knows Mamá thinks of Him as she thinks of Ernesto, and the way the days feel longer with his absence.

"Mamí," Sandra says, "I pray for him every night. Even before—"

"Sí, mijita." When Mamá speaks, her voice is softer than usual. "Lo sé."

Lo sé. It's one of those mundane phrases that often bothers Sandra. Mamá seems to always know more than she lets on. When Mamá says, "Lo sé," she's really saying something else. Something she's unwilling to articulate in the moment.

Mamá and Sandra kneel before the kitchen window and bow their heads together, clasping their hands to their foreheads. They haven't done this in a while. Mamá had given Sandra her first rosary, lilac with plastic beads that looked like a child strung it together. Sandra has since worn the lilac down to white from the pressure of her left thumb. When Ernesto had stopped visiting Mamá so frequently and started crashing at Sandra's—when he and Christie would get into fights or when he just wanted a meal or to talk and not have anyone ask too many questions—Mamá stopped insisting that Sandra come to church with her, stopped praying with her over Thursday dinners and all the other meals that Mamá decided to schedule last minute. "¿Caldo de pollo o carne en su jugo?" she would ask, and Sandra would almost always reply, "Carne en su jugo," because she loved the way her insides warmed as she spooned layers of carrots and chile and tender beef into her body. Ernesto would have never done something so vulnerable like bow his head before an open glass, or close his eyes to the rest of the world.

What do their hands reach for? The back door? The splintered wood on the cabinets? The spirit they feel there, pushing back at them through the windowpane? Something intangible. And bitter. Sandra wonders if Mamá can taste the salt in the air, too. She swears it hadn't been there before. The wind picks up outside and enters through the window. Sandra and Mamá sit in silence as the air fills the room. The house expands like an accordion to fill the heaviness of their souls. And when they whisper, "Amen," the house sighs with them.

Days

Sylvia WATANABE

Here is Mother in the sunlight, laughing—her red mouth, her pretty teeth. Here she is with Father, hand in hand, lying down upon the sea. And here, my not-yet mother on the day of her wedding to my not-yet father: she is wearing a yellow sundress, blonde curls spilling out beneath the wide brim of her hat; he is decorous in a borrowed suit. They are sitting in the front seat of a red convertible garlanded with paper flowers. The top is down, the day is fine, they are pleased with themselves and with each other.

I studied the photo, missing myself.

"But where am I?" I asked my father.

He pointed to a place just outside a lower corner. "There, seeing everything," he said. "Just smell those flowers."

I breathed in. I smelled the flowers.

My mother said I'd held my breath since I was born, that I came out blue from nearly drowning in the womb. "You were never a swimmer," my mother said. She claimed to have acquired the habit of wakefulness from sitting up with me on asthma nights, my father off again somewhere, administering the public health. Until I learned to breathe, she claimed, her hands were always there, holding me up while I was drowning, dispensing eucalyptus steam, honey tea, oxygen from a cylinder.

But I remember other nights, when it was not asthma keeping us awake, I'd slip from my bed and follow the light into the kitchen where she was already pouring the steaming chocolate into cups, two places set at the table.

I'd say, "It looks like you're expecting someone."

She'd smile and hand me the buttered toast, which we spread with honey from the wild beehives in the Keawe woods. There, in that honeyed light, she was still the doctor's wife. A pair of eyes, a pair of hands.

She said, without her seeing to it, he'd have given all his time away—he'd give free medical advice, the last piece of pie, the dancing ladies from her garden. On weekday mornings if she was not at the door to see him off, he called to her, "Where are you Eva," as if he had misplaced something he could not do without.

My mother did not tell me stories. She read me the news. She read about a place in England where, each year, it rained green beans in the summertime. She read about a woman in New Mexico who discovered the face of Jesus on a tortilla and a famous poet who wrote a poem about this. She read about a boy with gills who lived underwater and a woman who gave birth to a jellyfish. She read about a dog in Russia, swallowed by a giant sturgeon which was then pulled from the river and slit open.

The dog, released, was quite itself again.

"Everyone can use a second chance at life," my mother said. It was she who named me Lazarus.

Koya, Rose Lazarus Bright. My name is in my mother's hands. It is on thick paper, neatly typed. We skip down past the date and hour of birth to the names and colors—

Mother's Full Maiden Name: Bright, Evelyn St. Lazarre
Race: White
Father's Name: Koya, Franklin Hiroshi
Race: O ther

Between the O and the t, there is a small gray smudge, and, faintly showing through, the trace of letters that I can't make out.

She was fresh out of library school when they met (*Come home, why don't you come home*, they told her, but she wouldn't hear it), and he was all the way from Hawayah, training as a doctor in America. My mother's version is spare on detail—all that bright hair, that clear skin; she could light any room she was in.

And then, one day, she lit on him.

It would have been one of those sudden days when winter gives way to spring—the air filled with ease, the bulbs tricked into blooming.

"Evvy Bright, you watch your step!" her mother warned.

"Yes, dancing!" Little Evvy (now Eva) said.

Memories like fishes, slippery, fast. My father with a butterfly net. My father in a funny hat. My father reading aloud, Once there was a girl who lived under the sea—

In Father's version, they met in a book. A night of no-sleep, prowling the dim-lit stacks of the library. Somewhere between *picornaviridae* and *retroviridae*, he happened to glance up and there she was. It was morning, and she was standing in a ray of winter sun. "Hello," she said. "My name is Evelyn."

She was also known as Evvy, Lina, Lindy, Lynn. "Someday you will grow into your proper name," her mother had said.

But Eva came to be her best name, a knife's edge on a daughter's tongue; it was the name I did not say aloud (she was always Mother), the name she was called, my father said, by all the men who loved her.

Eva, he says. Eva, Eva, Eva—

If you know the name of a thing, you know what it is, my father believed. In his books, which he called keys, were the names of every kind of plant and animal and their medical significance. These are the names he taught me: order, family, genus, species.

There must be order in a family; everything belongs to a genus, a species.

On weekends, when he was not called away by work, my father and I went for naming walks. For my eighth birthday, he gave me a clothbound notebook with waterproof pages, like the one he carried everywhere. In his he kept an illustrated record of all the scientific things he had observed. On the cover of mine he'd printed, *A Book of Names*.

The early entries are in his hand; the pictures that accompany them are mine. *Anura*. A green-skinned woman with spectacles. *Lepidoptera*. A gaudy angel. *Odonata, megaloptera*—each name calling up weather, a particular day and place.

On green days, smelling of fern, it rains in the woods; we rescue damsels from the lake.

On gray days, swelling with heat, we hunt red dragons among the cattails.

On blue summer days, the sky the color of pigment squeezed from a tube, the milkweed crawls with fat black and yellow caterpillars.

My father and I collected other things too, things we brought into the house, despite my mother's admonitions.

Poison ivy from the woods. A bucket of crawdads that escaped behind the stove before we could boil them for supper. Strands of marsh pearls which turned into tadpoles, and then one morning, into small green frogs which we found all over the house for days.

Some weekends we packed sandwiches and drinks into a canvas satchel and went for naming walks in our backyard.

"You do not have to go far to find new things," he said, pointing out the ant lion dens beneath the lilacs, the wood bees nesting in the compost bin.

The specimens we did not keep alive went into the killing jar, layered at the bottom with crushed cyanide covered with plaster of Paris. These we dried for pinning in a cork-lined box. The ones my father could not identify by sight he looked up in one of his insect keys.

Evelyna evanae has five stingers on each hand and one on the tip of her tongue. Her antennae are silver laments; her rain-colored eyes are neither green nor blue nor gray. She flies by night, invisible in the light of day.

One afternoon, I found my father in his study, searching the titles upon his shelves. There was an open book in his hands and other books lying open upon his desk, pages marked with notes.

"—The Morphology of Insects, Linnaean Systems, Trapp's guide to Medically Significant Arthropods—" He turned to me, reciting titles. "Soon we must learn all of this new."

When I asked why, he said that a new system of naming was being invented—a system based on DNA.

"But what is DNA? Why can't we keep the old names too?" I asked.

"The old names will still be there," he said. "They are useful for naming the outside of things. But the new names look *under* —at what cannot be seen."

Just as weekends were my favorite days, my father's study was my favorite place. Here, I spent the long hours when he was away, and asthma kept me home from school, browsing his books and poking through his enormous desk.

There, in secret drawers and cubbies, he always left treasure for me to find. Three tiny mongoose skulls covered with miniscule writing, a rubber stamp in a metal box containing a piece of night sky, a sea-green insect's wing in a covered jar—

> *This wing, he explains, belongs to a rare and very beautiful moth, called the Fabulous Green Sphinx. It lives only in the tops of certain trees on the highest mountains of the tropical islands where he grew up. Very few people have ever seen one, much less captured an intact specimen, and when he was a boy, it was his dream to travel to the rain forest and watch them fly.*
>
> *When I ask if he did, he does not answer. He has turned to the*

window and is gazing at Mother out in the garden. Slowly, she moves among the rows of flowers with a basket and a pair of shears. She sees us and waves, the sunlight shining through the gauzy fabric of her summer dress, her sleeves fluttering in the breeze.

At any moment, she will lift into the air, it seems.

CONTRI-BUTORS

Hanif ABDURRAQIB is a writer from the east side of Columbus, Ohio.

Ruth AWAD is the Lebanese-American author of *Set to Music a Wildfire*, winner of the 2016 Michael Waters Poetry Prize and 2018 Ohioana Book Award for Poetry.

S. Erin BATISTE is the author of the chapbook, *Glory to All Fleeting Things*. Her poems appear in *Cosmonauts Avenue*, *Paper Darts*, *Peach Mag*, and *Puerto del Sol*, among other journals.

Abigail CHABITNOY is the author of *How to Dress a Fish* (Wesleyan). She is a Koniag descendant and member of the Tangirnaq Native Village in Kodiak.

K-Ming CHANG is a Kundiman fellow and Lambda Literary Award finalist. Her poetry has been anthologized in *Ink Knows No Borders*, *Bettering American Poetry Vol. 3*, and the *Pushcart Prize Anthology*.

Leila CHATTI is a Tunisian-American poet and author of *Deluge* and the chapbooks *Tunsiya/Amrikiya* and *Ebb*.

Chen CHEN is the author of *When I Grow Up I Want to Be a List of Further Possibilities* (BOA Editions and Bloodaxe Books). He teaches at Brandeis University.

Nina Li COOMES is a Japanese and American writer, currently living in Chicago. Her work has appeared in *The Atlantic*, *Catapult*, and *Eater,* among other places.

Kyle DACUYAN is a poet, performance-maker, and the Executive Director of The Poetry Project at St. Mark's.

Geffrey DAVIS is the author of *Night Angler* (BOA Editions) and *Revising the Storm* (BOA Editions). He teaches with the University of Arkansas and The Rainier Writing Workshop.

Dalton DAY is a preschool teacher and lives in Georgia.

Shastra DEO is a poet and editor living in Brisbane. Her first book, *The Agonist* (UQP), won the 2018 Australian Literature Society Gold Medal.

Theophilus KWEK has published five volumes of poetry, and has been shortlisted twice for the Singapore Literature Prize.

Peter LABERGE is author of the chapbooks *Makeshift Cathedral* (YesYes Books) and *Hook* (Sibling Rivalry Press). He is the founder and editor-in-chief of *The Adroit Journal.*

Tariq LUTHUN is an analyst, community organizer, and Emmy Award-winning poet from Detroit. A diasporic Palestinian, he received his MFA from Warren Wilson College.

Dr. Irène P. MATHIEU is a pediatrician and writer. She is the author of *Grand Marronage* (Switchback Books), *orogeny* (Trembling Pillow Press), and *the galaxy of origins* (dancing girl press).

Anis MOJGANI is an American poet and artist from New Orleans. He likes sweet coffee and lives in Portland, Oregon, where he is currently working on picture books.

Mary MUSSMAN is a doctoral candidate in Comparative Literature at the University of California, Berkeley. Her poetry can be found in *fields*, *Pacifica Literary Review*, *Hypocrite Reader*, and elsewhere.

Patricia Patterson is an MFA candidate at UNC Greensboro and a fiction editor for *The Greensboro Review*. Her work is featured in *Pank*, *Longleaf Review*, and *Cotton Xenomorph*, among others.

Janel PINEDA is a Los-Angeles born poet, activist, and the daughter of Salvadoran immigrants.

Jeremy RADIN is a poet, actor, and teacher. He lives in Los Angeles where he once sat next to Carly Rae Jepsen in a restaurant.

David ROMPF has written for *The New York Times*, *Harvard Review*, *The Common*, *The Los Angeles Times*, *Newsweek*, and many other publications. He lives in New York City.

Omar SAKR is an award-winning Arab Australian poet. His books include *These Wild Houses* (Cordite), and *The Lost Arabs*

(UQP), out now in Australia and soon in the US.

Raena SHIRALI is the author of *Gilt* (YesYes Books). Shirali lives in Philadelphia, where she is an Assistant Professor of English at Holy Family University.

Clint SMITH is the author of the poetry collection *Counting Descent* and the forthcoming narrative nonfiction book *How the Word Is Passed*. He is a PhD candidate at Harvard University.

Maggie SMITH's most recent poetry collection is *Good Bones*. Her poems and essays appear in the *The New York Times*, *The Paris Review*, *Tin House*, *The Believer*, and *The New Yorker*.

Bethany SWANN is a PhD student in English at UPenn exploring spiritual identity and material culture in Asian diasporas.

An UONG's work is forthcoming or has appeared in *Eater*, *Catapult*, *Boston Globe Magazine*, *Roads and Kingdoms*, *Winter Tangerine*, and elsewhere. She can't say no to a bowl of bún bò Huế.

Marco YAN's poems have appeared in *Diode*, *The Adroit Journal*, *The Arkansas International*, among other places. He currently lives and teaches in Hong Kong.

Sylvia WATANABE is a writer and comics artist who lives in Michigan. She is the author of the collection *Talking to the Dead*.

WITH THANKS